I0805190

# What Do Firefighters Do?

ROLES IN MY COMMUNITY

Leigh McClure

CIVICS FOR THE REAL WORLD™

Rosen Classroom™

Firefighters work at the fire hall.

Firefighters can be men
or women.
They are very brave.

Firefighters put out fires.

They wear coats and helmets.

They drive big fire trucks.

Firefighters save people who are in trouble.

# WORDS TO KNOW

coat

fire hall

fire truck

helmet